MR. JELLY
and the Pirates

Original concept by
Roger Hargreaves

Written and illustrated by
Adam Hargreaves

Mr Jelly is the most nervous person you will ever meet. The slightest thing will send him into a panic.

Even the sound of the wind in the trees will make him bolt behind the sofa, quivering and shaking in fear.

So as you can imagine, it takes Mr Jelly a long time to pluck up enough courage to go on holiday.

This year, Mr Jelly went to Seatown.

Mr Jelly longed to join everyone playing in the sea, but he was too frightened.

"Why don't you go for a swim?" suggested Mr Lazy.

"I . . . I'm too scared," admitted Mr Jelly. "There might be nasty seaweed . . . or a crab . . . or . . . or a shark!"

"Well, why don't you go out in my dinghy?" replied Mr Lazy.

"I . . . I . . . might drift out to sea and never be found again," said Mr Jelly, trembling at the thought.

"No you won't," said Mr Lazy. "Not if I hold on to the rope."

Mr Jelly thought this over and decided to risk it.

After a while, Mr Jelly began to enjoy himself in the dinghy. But when he looked back, he discovered that he was a very long way from the beach.

Mr Lazy had fallen asleep and the rope had slipped through his fingers!

"Oh help! Oh help! A wave is going to turn over the boat and I'm going to be swallowed by a whale!" shrieked Mr Jelly. But he was too far away for anyone to hear him.

Before long the land disappeared and large, black storm clouds gathered on the horizon.

Thunder boomed and lightning crackled. The sea rose up in a great roaring mass that tossed the little dinghy from wave to wave.

Mr Jelly cowered in the bottom of the boat.

"Oh help! Oh help!" he shrieked. "I'm going to be struck by lightning, and burnt to a crisp, and tipped out of the boat and drowned!"

And then he fainted.

When he came to, he discovered that he had been washed up on to a tiny, deserted island.

Mr Jelly stared out at the vast expanse of sea.

"Oh help," he said in a very small voice, and then he fainted again.

Mr Jelly was woken by the sound of digging. He peered through the bushes at the side of the beach. What he saw filled him with terror . . .

Three swashbuckling, ruthless-looking pirates were digging up a treasure chest!

Mr Jelly knew that he must not make a sound, but the more he tried not to make a sound, the more he wobbled and trembled in fear. And the more he wobbled and trembled, the more the bushes shook and rustled.

So, in a very short time, Mr Jelly was found and set, quivering, on the sand in front of the pirates.

"Well, shiver my timbers, if he ain't just what we need," growled the pirate Captain. "A cabin boy!"

The three pirates and their new cabin boy rowed out to their ship, anchored in the bay.

Mr Jelly shook and trembled and quivered in terror.

The pirates, who prided themselves on their bravery, chuckled and laughed. They had never met anyone as nervous as Mr Jelly.

And over the following week, they came to realise just how nervous Mr Jelly really was.

On the first day, the first mate ordered Mr Jelly up into the rigging to set the sail.

"Oh help! Oh help!" shrieked Mr Jelly. "It's so high up and I'm going to have to climb and climb, and then I'll be even higher up, and I'll get dizzy, and I'll fall down into the sea and I'll be eaten by a shark!"

And then he fainted.

Luckily he had only climbed two rungs and the first mate caught him easily.

"I'd never thought of that," murmured the first mate to himself.

The next day, the quartermaster ordered Mr Jelly to sharpen the cutlasses on the grinding stone.

"Oh help! Oh help!" shrieked Mr Jelly. "I'll make the cutlass very sharp, and it will be so sharp that I will cut my finger, and then I'll bleed and bleed and . . ."

And then he fainted.

"I'd never thought of that," mumbled the quartermaster to himself.

On the third day, the gunner ordered Mr Jelly to practise firing the cannon.

"Oh help! Oh help!" shrieked Mr Jelly. "I'll load the cannon, and then fire the cannon and the explosion will be so loud that I'll go deaf, and then I won't be able to hear anything, and then . . ."

And then . . . well, you know what happened then.

He fainted.

Again.

"I'd never thought of that," muttered the gunner to himself.

And so it continued all week.

Mr Jelly even fainted when the cook ordered him to light the stove in the galley because he was afraid he would set the ship on fire!

And a very strange thing happened during the week.
Not only did the pirates discover how nervous
Mr Jelly was, but they also began to find out how
nervous they were, too.

The more Mr Jelly shrieked and fainted and quivered
and quaked at what terrible accidents might happen,
the more the pirates found themselves worrying.
By the end of the week, the pirate Captain found
himself with a crew who were too scared to do
anything.

Even the ship's carpenter had downed tools because
he was afraid he might get a splinter!

"This is hopeless!" roared the Captain. "How can we call ourselves pirates? That cabin boy has turned you all into scaredy cats. Mr Jelly must walk the plank!"

So, Mr Jelly was pushed out on to the plank.

"Oh help! Oh help!" shrieked Mr Jelly. "Don't make me walk the plank. I'll fall into the sea and then I'll have to swim for hours and hours and then I'll get weaker and weaker and then I'll drown!"

"That's horrible," said the first mate.

"Yeh, really nasty," agreed the quartermaster.

"We can't do that," said the gunner.

And the rest of the crew agreed.

"That's it!" cried the Captain. "I give up. Do what you want!"

And the crew did.

They sailed, very cautiously and very slowly, to Seatown, where they let Mr Jelly off.

Mr Jelly found Mr Lazy on the beach.

Fast asleep.

Mr Lazy yawned, stretched and opened an eye. "Hello," he said, sleepily. "Did you have fun? Sorry I fell asleep, but here you are safe and sound."

Mr Jelly began to wobble and quiver and shake.

But not in fear.

Mr Jelly was very, very, very angry!